To The Sawyers Bunch with Love, Juli

Boys Town, Nebraska

Gas Happens!

What to Do When It Happens to You

Written by
Julia Cook
Illustration by
Anita DuFalla

Gas Happens!

ISBN 978-1-934490-76-1

Published by the Boys Town Press
14100 Crawford St.
Boys Town, NE 68010

For a Boys Town Press catalog, call **1-800-282-6657**
or visit our website: **BoysTownPress.org**

Publisher's Cataloging-in-Publication Data

Cook, Julia, 1964-

Gas happens! : what to do when it happens to you / written by Julia Cook ; illustrated by Anita DuFalla.
-- Boys Town, NE : Boys Town Press, c2015.

pages ; cm.
(Communicate with confidence)

ISBN: 978-1-934490-76-1

Summary: Did you know that everyone passes gas? If it's so natural, why do we struggle with teaching children how to respond appropriately? Join Gus in this hilarious tale as he and his classmates learn the brief biology lesson behind why we all pass gas, and the right way and the wrong way to handle it.--Publisher.

1. Gastrointestinal gas--Juvenile fiction. 2. Flatulence--Juvenile fiction. 3. Digestive organs--Juvenile fiction. 4. Gases--Physiological effect--Juvenile fiction. 5. Etiquette for children and teenagers--Juvenile fiction. 6. Children--Life skills guides. 7. [Gastrointestinal gas--Fiction. 8. Flatulence--Fiction. 9. Digestive organs--Fiction. 10. Gases--Fiction. 11. Behavior--Fiction. 12. Etiquette--Fiction. 13. Conduct of life.] I. DuFalla, Anita. II. Title. III. Series: Communicate with confidence ; no. 3.

PZ7.C76984 G37 2015

[E]--dc23 1502

Printed in the United States
10 9 8 7 6 5 4 3 2 1

Boys Town Press is the publishing division of Boys Town, a national organization serving children and families.

My name is **Gus…** but most people call me

"GAS."

I wish it was because I could run really fast,
but it's not… and I don't.

Yesterday at school, I was sitting in class working on my

10-Minute Math Marathon Speed Test.

We do them every morning, and I was doing great on mine!

But then I felt a bubble,
a bubble full of air.
It jiggled around inside me,
but I pretended I didn't care.

I wiggled around in my seat,
and readjusted my shirt.
But before I could stop the bubble,

I let out a great BIG burp!

"Gas leak!" said Garth. "Gross!" said Mary.
And everyone started to laugh.
"SHHHH!" *my teacher said.*
"I need you to finish your math!

Gas Happens!"

"Gus... I need you to say, EXCUSE ME!"

Then after lunch, I was taking my spelling test. We were all supposed to be quiet so everyone could think.

But I felt another bubble,
a bubble full of air.
It jiggled around inside me.
Was it the chili, the chips... or the pears?

I wiggled around in my seat,
and readjusted my shirt.
But before I could stop it, the bubble came out,
and I let out another BIG burp!

"Gas leak!" said Don. "Gross!" said Linda.

"SHHHH!" my teacher said.

"Keep working on your spelling tests.

I need everyone to do their best!

Gas Happens!"

"Gus, please say, (EXCUSE ME)!"

Then at the end of the day, during our personal silent reading time, it happened again… only this time, it was worse!

I felt another bubble,
a bubble full of air.
It jiggled around inside me,
but I pretended it wasn't there.

I wiggled around in my seat,
then I pulled on the side of my shoe.
But before I could stop it, the bubble came out,
only this time, it was a

toot!

TOOT

"Major gas leak!" said Jack. "Gross!" said Maxine.
Then everyone started to laugh.
"Keep reading," my teacher said,
"or I'll cut your recess in half!

Gas Happens!"

"Gus, please say, EXCUSE ME!"

This morning when I got on the bus, Barbara was wearing her **"Celebrate Our Clean Air Act"** t-shirt and she told everyone she wore it just for me.

When we got to school, we didn't take our

10-Minute Math Marathon Speed Test.

Instead, our teacher taught us a new lesson. She called it:

Gas Happens...

What to do When It Happens to You.

Then she said,

"Everyone and every living thing passes gas – *except* **jellyfish** *and* **coral sponges.** Gas Happens!"

"Every time you eat, drink or talk, you swallow air. This air turns into gas bubbles that float around inside your digestive tract. When your body breaks down the food you eat, even more gas bubbles are formed.

Gas bubbles can stay inside your body only for so long, and then they need to come out. When the gas bubbles come out of your body, you pass gas and pop the bubbles."

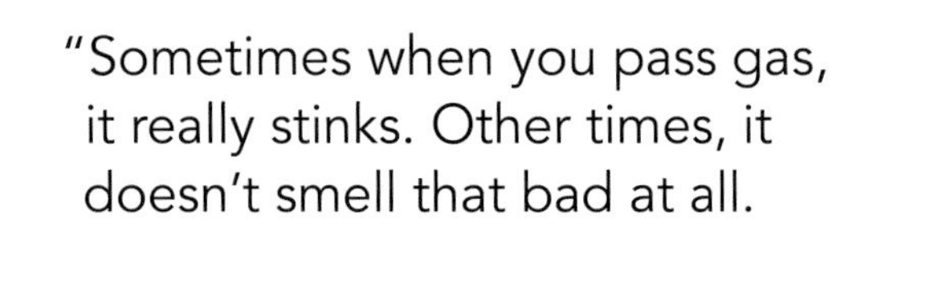

"Sometimes when you pass gas, it really stinks. Other times, it doesn't smell that bad at all.

Sometimes when you pass gas, it makes a loud noise. Other times, you can't even hear the bubbles pop."

"Sometimes, people pass gas on purpose.

But most of the time, they are just having a hard time controlling it.

Gas bubbles can be VERY tricky!"

"Some foods you eat can give you a lot of gas.

Everybody's digestive system is different, and different foods affect different people in different ways.

Chewing gum can give you gas because when you chew it, you swallow a lot of air.

Just remember… everyone and every living thing gets gas and has to pass it – *except* jellyfish *and* coral sponges."

"Did you know that each and every one of you (including me) passes gas at least

14 times a day?

Gas Happens!"

"From now on when we are in class,
and one of us passes gas,
remember, it happens to everyone,
and nobody needs to laugh.

Instead what you need to do,
to see this problem through,
is to breathe in, breathe out, smile and move on.
Just think... it could have been you!"

*"If you are the one who has gas,
remember there's a time and a place.
If you have a bubble that's on its way out,
do all you can to save face.*

Excuse yourself from the room.
Turn your head and cover your mouth.
And always say (EXCUSE ME)
if your gas bubble travels south."

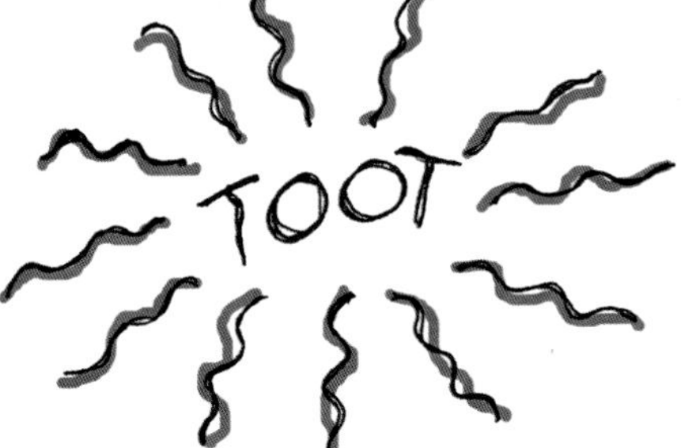

SOUTH

"Don't let a little gas bubble ruin what we need to do.

Breathe IN, breathe OUT, SMILE and move ON,

when gas is passed at school."

"You seriously want us to breathe in?" Barbara said. "That might not be such a great idea!"

"True!" my teacher said. "I think I need to add a step."

1. Turn your head.
2. Breathe in.
3. Breathe out.
4. Smile.
5. Move on.

This afternoon, it was our turn to have Betty Jean – the Read-To-Me dog – in our classroom. I was reading out loud to Betty Jean when…

She must have felt a bubble,
a bubble full of air.
It jiggled around inside her,
but she acted like she didn't care.

*She wiggled around on the floor,
and then she tugged at her fur.
But before she could stop it, the bubble came out.
But the bubble wasn't a burp!*

Gas Happened!

We all **turned our heads** (and wrinkled our noses!!!!).

Then we **breathed in, breathed out, smiled** and **moved on.**

I kept right on reading to Betty Jean because everyone and every living thing passes gas…
except jellyfish *and* coral sponges!

Now, we just need to figure out a way to teach Betty Jean to say, EXCUSE ME!

Tips for Parents and Educators

It May be a Tricky Subject, but Gas Happens!

Passing gas is a bodily function that affects all living things (except jellyfish and coral sponges). Knowing what to do, what to say and how to act when someone passes gas is a social skill that everyone effectively needs to master.

1 **Explain that everyone and every living thing** (except jellyfish and coral sponges) **passes gas. Experts say this happens at least 14 times a day...** Gas Happens!

2 **When someone else passes gas:**

- Turn your head.
- Breathe in.
- Breathe out.
- Smile.
- Move on.

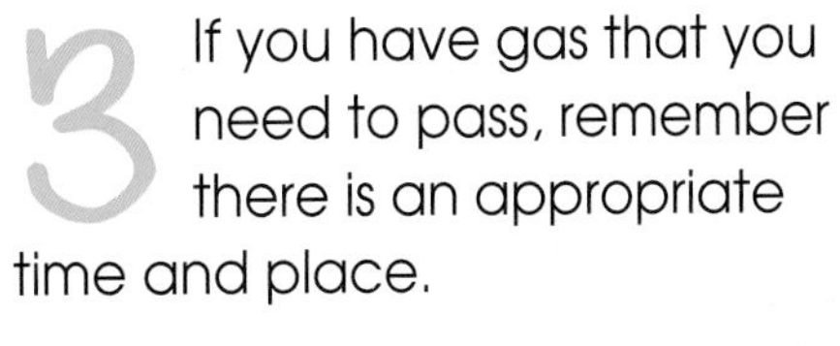

3 If you have gas that you need to pass, remember there is an appropriate time and place.

- If possible, excuse yourself from the room.
- Cover your mouth when you burp.
- Say EXCUSE ME when you burp or pass gas.
- Smile and move on (keep doing what you are doing) and always remember... Gas Happens!

For more parenting information, visit boystown.org/parenting.

Boys Town Press Books by Julia Cook

Kid-friendly books to teach social skills

A book series to help kids master the art of communicating.

978-1-934490-57-0

978-1-934490-58-7

978-1-934490-76-1

A book series to help kids get along.

978-1-934490-30-3

978-1-934490-39-6

978-1-934490-47-1

978-1-934490-48-8

978-1-934490-62-4

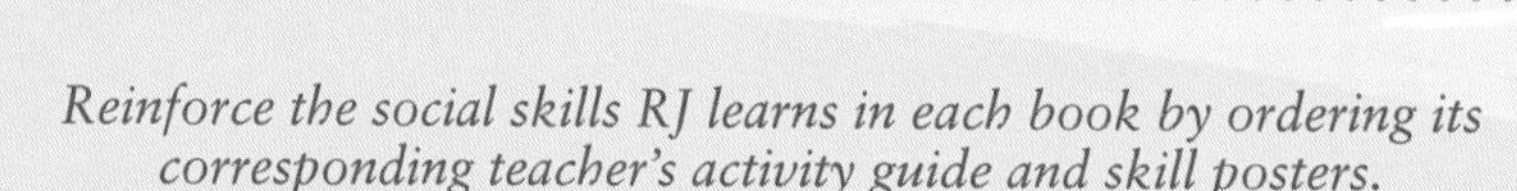

Reinforce the social skills RJ learns in each book by ordering its corresponding teacher's activity guide and skill posters.

978-1-934490-20-4
978-1-934490-34-1 (SPANISH)
978-1-934490-23-5 (ACTIVITY GUIDE)

978-1-934490-25-9
978-1-934490-53-2 (SPANISH)
978-1-934490-27-3 (ACTIVITY GUIDE)

978-1-934490-28-0
978-1-934490-32-7 (ACTIVITY GUIDE)

978-1-934490-35-8
978-1-934490-37-2 (ACTIVITY GUIDE)

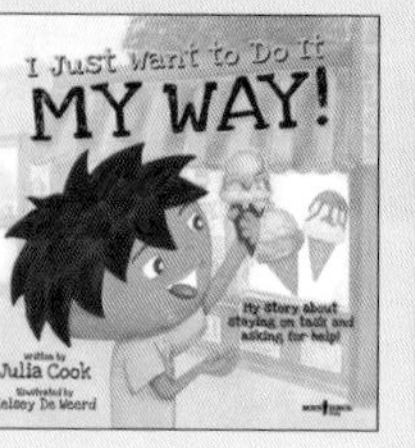

978-1-934490-43-3
978-1-934490-45-7 (ACTIVITY GUIDE)

978-1-934490-49-5
978-1-934490-51-8 (ACTIVITY GUIDE)

978-1-934490-67-9
978-1-934490-69-3 (AC

BoysTownPress.org

For information on Boys Town, its Education Model®, Common Sense Parenting® and training programs:
boystowntraining.org | boystown.org/parenting.org
training@BoysTown.org | 1-800-545-5771

For parenting and educational books and other resources:
BoysTownPress.org
btpress@BoysTown.org | 1-800-282-66